Robert Louis Stevenson

A Mountain Town in France

A Fragment

Robert Louis Stevenson

A Mountain Town in France
A Fragment

ISBN/EAN: 9783743350052

Manufactured in Europe, USA, Canada, Australia, Japa

Cover: Foto ©Andreas Hilbeck / pixelio.de

Manufactured and distributed by brebook publishing software
(www.brebook.com)

Robert Louis Stevenson

A Mountain Town in France

A MOUNTAIN TOWN IN FRANCE

Illustration I.

Panorama from Morel's at Le Monastier.

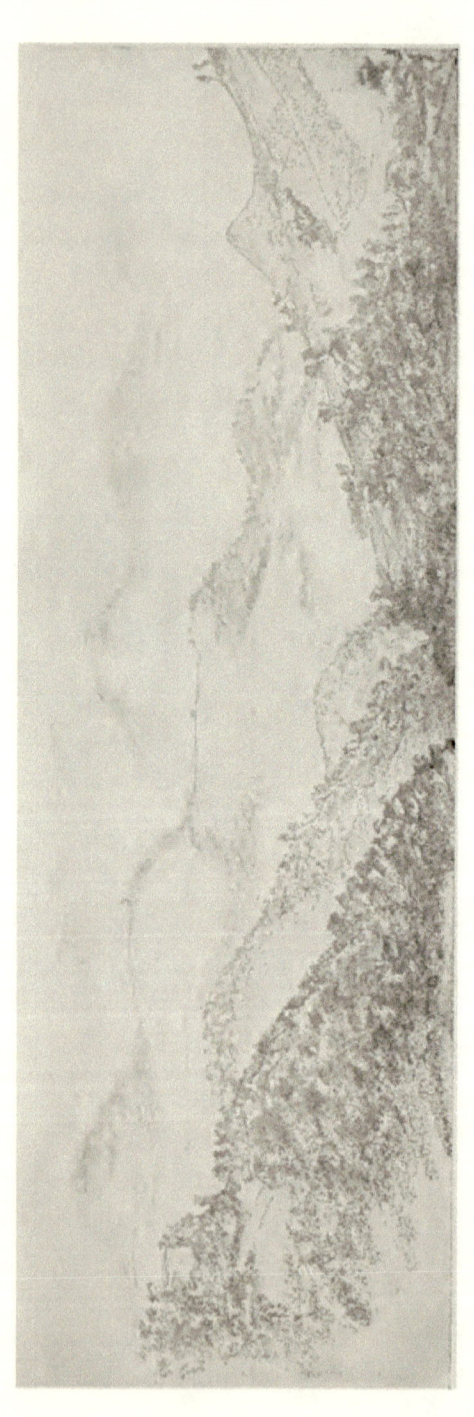

A Mountain Town in France

A FRAGMENT BY

ROBERT LOUIS STEVENSON

With Five Illustrations
by the Author

JOHN LANE : THE BODLEY HEAD
NEW YORK AND LONDON
1896

WE are indebted to the representatives of the late Robert Louis Stevenson for permission to print the following account of his stay at Le Monastier in the autumn of 1878. It was intended to serve as the opening chapter of his well-known volume, *Travels with a Donkey in the Cevennes;* but the intention was abandoned in favour of a more abrupt beginning, and the fragment is now printed for the first time.

It is published in America by arrangement with the proprietor of *The Studio.*

LIST OF ILLUSTRATIONS

A Mountain Town in France

LE MONASTIER is the chief place of a hilly can-
ton in Haute Loire, the ancient Velay. As the
name betokens, the town is of monastic origin ;
and it still contains a towered bulk of monastery
and a church of some architectural pretensions,
the seat of an arch-priest and several vicars. It
stands on the side of a hill above the river Gazeille,
about fifteen miles from Le Puy, up a steep road
where the wolves sometimes pursue the diligence
in winter. The road, which is bound for Vivarais,
passes through the town from end to end in a single narrow street ; there you may see the fountain
where women fill their pitchers ; there also some
old houses with carved doors and pediments and
ornamental work in iron. For Monastier, like
Maybole in Ayrshire, was a sort of country capi-
tal, where the local aristocracy had their town
mansions for the winter; and there is a certain
baron still alive and, I am told, extremely penitent,
who found means to ruin himself by high living
in this village on the hills. He certainly has
claims to be considered the most remarkable

spendthrift on record.   How he set about it, in a
place where there are no luxuries for sale, and
where the board at the best inn comes to little
more than a shilling a day, is a problem for the
wise.   His son, ruined as the family was, went as
far as Paris to sow his wild oats ; and so the cases
of father and son mark an epoch in the history of
centralization in France.   Not until the latter had
got into the train was the work of Richelieu
complete.

It is a people of lace-makers.   The women sit
in the streets by groups of five or six, and the
noise of the bobbins is audible from one group to
another.   Now and then you will hear one woman
clattering off prayers for the edification of the
others at their work.   They wear gaudy shawls,
white caps with a gay ribbon about the head, and
sometimes a black felt brigand hat above the cap ;
and so they give the street colour and brightness
and a foreign air.   A while ago, when England
largely supplied herself from this district with the
lace called *torchon*, it was not unusual to earn five
francs a day ; and five francs in Monastier is worth
a pound in London.   Now, from a change in the
market, it takes a clever and industrious work-
woman to earn from three to four in the week, or
less than an eighth of what she made easily a few
years ago.   The tide of prosperity came and went,
as with our northern pitmen, and left nobody the
richer.   The women bravely squandered their

Illustration II.

Lantriac.

Lantivic

gains, kept the men in idleness, and gave themselves up, as I was told, to sweethearting and a
merry life. From week's end to week's end it was
one continuous gala in Monastier ; people spent
the day in the wine-shops, and the drum or the
bag-pipes led on the *bourrées* up to ten at night.
Now these dancing days are over. " *Il n'y a plus de
jeunesse*," said Victor the garçon. I hear of no
great advance in what are thought the essentials
of morality ; but the *bourrée*, with its rambling,
sweet, interminable music, and alert and rustic fig-
ures, has fallen into disuse, and is mostly remem-
bered as a custom of the past. Only on the
occasion of the fair shall you hear a drum dis-
creetly rattling in a wine-shop, or perhaps one of
the company singing the measure while the others
dance. I am sorry at the change, and marvel
once more at the complicated scheme of things
upon this earth, and how a turn of fashion in England can silence so much mountain merriment in
France. The lace-makers themselves have not
entirely forgiven our country-women ; and I think
they take a special pleasure in the legend of the
northern quarter of the town, called L'Anglade,
because there the English free lances were ar-
rested and driven back by the potency of a little
Virgin Mary on the wall.

From time to time a market is held, and the
town has a season of revival ; cattle and pigs are
stabled in the streets ; and pickpockets have been

known to come all the way from Lyons for the
occasion.   Every Sunday the country folk throng
in with daylight to buy apples, to attend mass and
to visit one of the wine-shops, of which there are
no less than fifty in this little town.   Sunday-wear
for the men is a green tail coat of some coarse
sort of drugget, and usually a complete suit to
match.   I have never set eyes on such degrading
raiment.   Here it clings, there bulges ; and the
human body, with its agreeable and lively lines, is
turned into a mockery and laughing-stock.   Another piece of Sunday business with the peasants
is to take their ailments to the chemist for advice.
It is as much a matter for Sunday as church-go-
ing.   I have seen a woman who had been unable
to speak since the Monday before, wheezing,
catching her breath, endlessly and painfully cough-
ing ; and yet she had waited upwards of a hundred
hours before coming to seek help, and had the
week been twice as long, she would have waited
still.   There was a canonical day for consultation ;
such was the ancestral habit, to which a respect-
able lady must study to conform.

Two conveyances go daily to Le Puy, but they
rival each other in polite concessions rather than
in speed.   Each will wait an hour or two hours
cheerfully while an old lady does her marketing
or a gentleman finishes the papers in a café.   The
Courier (such is the name of one) should leave
Le Puy by two in the afternoon on the return

voyage, and arrive at Monastier in good time for
a six o'clock dinner. But the driver dares not
disoblige his customers. He will postpone his
departure again and again, hour after hour; and
I have known the sun to go down on his delay.
These purely personal favours, this consideration
of men's fancies, rather than the hands of a
mechanical clock, as marking the advance of the
abstraction, time, makes a more humorous business of stage coaching than we are used to
see it.

As far as the eye can reach, one swelling line
of hill-top rises and falls behind another; and if
you climb an eminence, it is only to see new and
further ranges behind these. Many little rivers
run from all sides in cliffy valleys; and one of
them, a few miles from Monastier, bears the great
name of Loire. The mean level of the country is
a little more than three thousand feet above the
sea, which makes the atmosphere proportionably
brisk and wholesome. There is little timber ex-
cept pines, and the greater part of the country
lies in moorland pasture. The country is wild
and tumbled rather than commanding; an upland
rather than a mountain district; and the most
striking as well as the most agreeable scenery lies
low beside the rivers. There, indeed, you will
find many corners that take the fancy; such as
made the English noble choose his grave by a
Swiss streamlet, where nature is at her freshest

and looks as young as on the seventh morning.
Such a place is the course of the Gazeille, where
it waters the common of Monastier and thence
downward till it joins the Loire—a place to hear
birds singing ; a place for lovers to frequent. The
name of the river was perhaps suggested by the
sound of its passage over the stones ; for it is a
great warbler, and at night, after I was in bed in
Monastier, I could hear it go singing down the
valley till I fell asleep.

On the whole, this is a Scottish landscape,
although not so noble as the best in Scotland ;
and by an odd coincidence, the population is, in
its way, as Scottish as the country. They have
abrupt, uncouth, Fifeshire manners, and accost
you, as if you were trespassing, with an " *Oùst-ce
que vous allez ?* " only translateable into the Low-
land " Whau'r ye gaun ?" They keep the Scottish
Sabbath.   There is no labour done on that day
but to drive in and out the various pigs and sheep
and cattle that make so pleasant a tinkling in the
meadows. The lace-makers have disappeared
from the street. Not to attend mass would in-
volve social degradation ; and you may find people reading Sunday books, in particular a sort
of Catholic *Monthly Visitor* on the doings of our
Lady of Lourdes. I remember one Sunday when
I was walking in the country that I fell on a
hamlet and found all the inhabitants, from the
patriarch to the baby, gathered in the shadow of

Illustration III.

Chateau Neuf, from the Gazeille.

a gable at prayer. One strapping lass stood with
her back to the wall and did the solo part, the rest
chiming in devoutly. Not far off a lad lay flat
on his face asleep, among some straw, to represent
the worldly element.

Again, this people is eager to proselytise ; and
the postmaster's daughter used to argue with me
by the half-hour about my heresy, until she grew
quite flushed. I have heard the reverse process
going on between a Scotswoman and a French
girl ; and the arguments in the two cases were
identical. Each apostle based her claim on the
superior virtue and attainments of her clergy, and
clinched the business with a threat of hell fire.
"*Pas bong prêtres ici,*" said the Presbyterian,
"*bong prêtres en Ecosse.*" And the postmaster's
daughter, taking up the same weapon, plied me,
so to speak, with the butt of it instead of the
bayonet. We are a hopeful race, it seems, and
easily persuaded for our good. One cheerful cir-
cumstance I note in these guerrilla missions, that
each side relies on hell, and Protestant and
Catholic alike address themselves to a supposed
misgiving in their adversary's heart. And I call
it cheerful, for faith is a more supporting quality
than imagination.

Here, as in Scotland, many peasant families
boast a son in holy orders. And here, also, the
young men have a tendency to emigrate. It is
certainly not poverty that drives them to the great

cities or across the seas; for many peasant families,
I was told, have a fortune of at least 40,000 francs.
The lads go forth pricked with the spirit of ad-
venture and the desire to rise in life, and leave
their homespun elders grumbling and wondering
over the event. Once, at a village called Laussonne, I met one of these disappointed parents;
a drake who had fathered a wild swan and seen it
take wing and disappear. The wild swan in question was now an apothecary in Brazil. He had
flown by way of Bordeaux, and first landed in
America, bare-headed and bare-foot, and with a
single half-penny in his pocket. And now he
was an apothecary! Such a wonderful thing is
an adventurous life! I thought he might as
well have stayed at home; but you never can tell
wherein a man's life consists, nor in what he sets
his pleasure: one to drink, another to marry, a third
to write scurrillous articles and be repeatedly caned
in public, and now this fourth, perhaps, to be an
apothecary in Brazil. As for his old father, he
could conceive no reason for the lad's behaviour.
"I had always bread for him," he said; "he ran
away to annoy me. He loved to annoy me. He
had no gratitude." But at heart he was swelling
with pride over his travelled offspring, and he
produced a letter out of his pocket where, as he
said, it was rotting, a mere lump of paper rags,
and waved it gloriously in the air. "This comes
from America," he cried, "six thousand leagues

Illustration IV.

In the Valley of the Laussonne.

in the valley of the Lauramne.

away!" And the wine-shop audience looked upon it with a certain thrill.

I soon became a popular figure, and was known for miles in the country. *Où'st-ce que vous allez?* was changed for me into *Quoi, vous rentrez au Monastier ce soir?* and in the town itself every urchin seemed to know my name, although no living creature could pronounce it. There was one particular group of lace-makers who brought out a chair for me whenever I went by, and detained me from my walk to gossip. They were filled with curiosity about England, its language, its religion, the dress of the women, and were never weary of seeing the queen's head on English postage stamps or seeking for French words in English journals. The language, in particular, filled them with surprise.

"Do they speak *patois* in England?" I was once asked; and when I told them not, "Ah, then, French?" said they.

"No, no," I said, "not French."

"Then," they concluded, "they speak *patois.*"

You must obviously either speak French or *patois.* Talk of the force of logic—here it was in all its weakness. I gave up the point, but proceeding to give illustrations of my native jargon, I was met with a new mortification. Of all *patois* they declared that mine was the most preposterous and the most jocose in sound. At each new word there was a new explosion of laughter, and

some of the younger ones were glad to rise from
their chairs and stamp about the street in ecstasy ;
and I looked on upon their mirth in a faint and
slightly disagreeable bewilderment. " Bread,"
which sounds a commonplace, plain-sailing mono-
syllable in England, was the word that most
delighted these good ladies of Monastier ; it
seemed to them frolicsome and racy, like a page
of Pickwick ; and they all got it carefully by
heart, as a stand-by, I presume, for winter even-
ings. I have tried it since then with every sort
of accent and inflection, but I seem to lack the
sense of humour.

They were of all ages : children at their first
web of lace, a stripling girl with a bashful but
encouraging play of eyes, solid married women,
and grandmothers, some on the top of their age
and some failing towards decrepitude. One and
all were pleasant and natural, ready to laugh
and ready with a certain quiet solemnity when
that was called for by the subject of our talk.
Life, since the fall in wages, had begun to appear
to them with a more serious air. The stripling
girl would sometimes laugh at me in a provoca-
tive and not unadmiring manner, if I judge
aright ; and one of the grandmothers, who was my
great friend of the party, gave me many a sharp
word of judgment on my sketches, my heresy, or
even my arguments, and gave them with a wry
mouth and a humorous twinkle in her eye that

were eminently Scottish. But the rest used me
with a certain reverence, as something come from
afar and not entirely human. Nothing would put
them at their ease but the irresistible gaiety of
my native tongue. Between the old lady and
myself I think there was a real attachment. She
was never weary of sitting to me for her portrait,
in her best cap and brigand hat, and with all her
wrinkles tidily composed; and though she never
failed to repudiate the result, she would always
insist upon another trial. It was as good as a
play to see her sitting in judgment over the last.
"No, no," she would say, "that is not it. I am
old, to be sure, but I am better looking than that.
We must try again." When I was about to leave
she bade me good-bye for this life in a somewhat
touching manner. We should not meet again,
she said; it was a long farewell, and she was
sorry. But life is so full of crooks, old lady, that
who knows? I have said good-bye to people for
greater distances and times, and, please God, I
mean to see them yet again.

One thing was notable about these women from
the youngest to the oldest, and with hardly an ex-
ception. In spite of their piety, they could twang
off an oath with Sir Toby Belch in person. There
was nothing so high or so low, in heaven or earth
or in the human body, but a woman of this neigh-
borhood would whip out the name of it, fair and
square, by way of conversational adornment. My

landlady, who was pretty and young, dressed like
a lady and avoided *patois* like a weakness, com-
monly addressed her child in the language of a
drunken bully. And of all the swearers that I
ever heard, commend me to an old lady in Gondet,
a village of the Loire. I was making a sketch,
and her curse was not yet ended when I had
finished it and took my departure. It is true she
had a right to be angry; for here was her son, a
hulking fellow, visibly the worse for drink before
the day was well begun. But it was strange to
hear her unwearying flow of oaths and obscenities,
endless like a river, and now and then rising to a
passionate shrillness in the clear and silent air of
the morning. In city slums, the thing might have
passed unnoticed; but in a country valley, and
from a plain and honest countrywoman, this beast-
liness of speech surprised the ear.

The *Conductor*, as he is called, of *Roads and
Bridges*, was my principal companion. He was
generally intelligent, and could have spoken more
or less falsetto on any of the trite topics; but it
was his specialty to have a generous taste in eating.
This was what was most indigenous in the man;
it was here he was an artist; and I found in his
company what I had long suspected, that enthu-
siasm and special knowledge are the great social
qualities, and what they are about, whether white
sauce or Shakespeare's plays, an altogether sec-
ondary question.

Illustration V.

Chateau Beaufort, from Gondet sur Loire.

I used to accompany the *Conductor* on his professional rounds, and grew to believe myself an expert in the business. I thought I could make an entry in a stonebreakers' time-book, or order manure off the wayside with any living engineer in France. Gondet was one of the places we visited together ; and Laussonne, where I met the apothecary's father, was another. There, at Laussonne, George Sand spent a day while she was gathering materials for the " Marquis de Villemer ; " and I have spoken with an old man, who was then a child running about the inn kitchen, and who still remembers her with a sort of reverence. It appears that he spoke French imperfectly ; for this reason George Sand chose him for companion, and whenever he let slip a broad and picturesque phrase in *patois*, she would make him repeat it again and again till it was graven in her memory. The word for a frog particularly pleased her fancy ; and it would be curious to know if she afterwards employed it in her works. The peasants, who knew nothing of letters and had never so much as heard of local colour, could not explain her chattering with this backward child ; and to them she seemed a very homely lady and far from beautiful : the most famous man-killer of the age appealed so little to Velaisian swine-herds !

On my first engineering excursion, which lay up by Crouzials toward Mount Mezenc and the borders of Ardèche, I began an improving ac-

quaintance with the foreman road-mender. He
was in great glee at having me with him, passed
me off among his subalterns as the supervising
engineer, and insisted on what he called "the
gallantry" of paying for my breakfast in a road-
side wine-shop. On the whole, he was a man of
great weather-wisdom, some spirits and a social
temper. But I am afraid he was superstitious.
When he was nine years old, he had seen one
night a company of *bourgeois et dames qui fai-
saient le manége avec des chaises*, and concluded
that he was in the presence of a witches' Sabbath.
I suppose, but venture with timidity on the sug-
gestion, that this may have been a romantic and
nocturnal picnic party. Again, coming from Pra-
delles with his brother, they saw a great, empty
cart, drawn by six enormous horses before them
on the road. The driver cried aloud and filled
the mountains with the cracking of his whip. He
never seemed to go faster than a walk, yet it was
impossible to overtake him ; and at length, at the
corner of a hill, the whole equipage disappeared
bodily into the night. At the time people said it
was the devil *qui s'amusait à faire ça.*

I suggested there was nothing more likely, as
he must have some amusement.

The foreman said it was odd, but there was less
of that sort of thing than formerly. "*C'est diffi-
cile*," he added, " *à expliquer.*"

When we were well up on the moors and the

Conductor was trying some road metal with the gauge—

"Hark!" said the foreman, "do you hear nothing?"

We listened, and the wind, which was blowing chilly out of the east, brought a faint, tangled jangling to our ears.

"It is the flocks of Vivarais," said he.

For every summer, the flocks out of all Ardèche are brought up to pasture on these grassy plateaux.

Here and there a little private flock was being tended by a girl, one spinning with a distaff, another seated on a wall and intently making lace. This last, when we addressed her, leaped up in a panic and put out her arms, like a person swimming, to keep us at a distance, and it was some seconds before we could persuade her of the honesty of our intentions.

The *Conductor* told me of another herdswoman from whom he had once asked his road while he was yet new to the country, and who fled from him, driving her beasts before her, until he had given up the information in despair. A tale of old lawlessness may yet be read in these uncouth timidities.

The winter in these uplands is a dangerous and melancholy time. Houses are snowed up, and wayfarers lost in a flurry within hail of their own fireside. No man ventures abroad without meat

and a bottle of wine, which he replenishes at every
wine-shop; and even thus equipped he takes the
road with terror.   All day the family sits about
the fire in a foul and airless hovel, and equally
without work or diversion.   The father may carve
a rude piece of furniture, but that is all that will
be done until the spring sets in again, and along
with it the labours of the field.   It is not for
nothing that you find a clock in the meanest of
these mountain habitations.   A clock and an
almanac, you would fancy, were indispensable
in such a life.   .   .   .   .